libra season

LIBRA SEASON

poems by suprihmbé
edited by Émelyne Museaux

bbydoll press Chicago, IL *2018*

Published by **bbydoll press**
Chicago, IL
Twitter: @thotscholar
www.patreon.com/thotscholar

Copyright © 2018 by suprihmbé
All rights reserved. No part of this book may be reproduced in any form or by an electronic or mechanical means, including information storage and retrieval systems, without permission in writing from the publisher, except by a reviewer who may quote brief passages in a review. For more information, address: suprihmbe@gmail.com.

First paperback edition December 2018

Illustrations copyright © 2018 by suprihmbé
Book design by suprihmbé
Edited by Émelyne Museaux

For those who care: Body Typeface is LTC Caslon, Title/Heading Typeface is Fairy Tales, anything that isn't these is King's Caslon.

for mo, fatcake, & dewbaby

and you, who were loved.

"You looked at me then like you knew me, and I thought it really was Eden, and I couldn't take your eyes in because I was loving the hoof marks on your cheeks."

--Toni Morrison, Sula

CONTENTS

- FEELTRIP   XIV
- LIBRA SEASON (INTRO)   1
- EPIPHANY   2
- RESTING BITCH FACE   7
- THE CULT OF UNBOTHEREDNESS   9
- ADVENTURES IN PORNOLAND   10
- INTO WONDERLAND   12
- IF YOU SEE ME, WEEP (HUNGER STONE)   13
- BITTER BITCH   15
- HOW TO MAKE A VILLIAN   16
- BECOMING (THE DRAGON'S DAUGHTER)   21
- WHAT IMMA DO (INTERLUDE)   29
- WATERLOGGED   30
- WATER CHALLENGE   33
- A DATE & A DRAGON   39
- SPEAK EASY   45
- CAKE CITY   49
- WEAPONS   50
- BLOOD UNDER THE SKIN   52
- BUT WHEN I GET MY WINGS...   57
- THANK YOU   58

FEELTRIP

by NOA
2 hr 56 min

I made this playlist after losing someone I love/d. The mood of the songs documents my feelings throughout that entire relationship, from beginning to end. I rediscovered certain parts of myself during that time and the following content is reflective of that growth. You are welcome to shuffle but I would suggest to first listen to them in this order and get lost in the journey. The list is available on Spotify as "feeltrip (libra season)" for your listening pleasure.[1]

Rebel Girl
Bikini Kill

Jenny
Studio Killers

Only a Girl
Gia

Cool for the Summer
Demi Lovato

Sleepover
Hayley Kiyoko

Nights With You
MØ

Playinwitme
KYLE, Kehlani

What I Need
Hayley Kiyoko, Kehlani

---

[1] Link: https://open.spotify.com/playlist/1LoIZxiy6Qcqmk2xDkC5J7

Honey
Kehlani

When it's Right
Alyson Stoner

I Know A Place
MUNA

Love Me Right
Amber Mark

Thinkin Bout You
Frank Ocean

PULL UP
ABRA

So High
Doja Cat

D'Evils
SiR

Honeywheat
Girl

Girlfriend
Nao

Dive
Tiffany Gouché

All the Way Down
Kelela

Gonna Love Me
Teyana Taylor

Make it Out Alive
Nao, SiR

W/As My Girl
Maxwell

Fool For You
Snoh Aalegra

Closer (Ode 2 U)
Ravyn Lenae

Ur
SZA

U Go I Go
ABRA

Waiting Game
Banks

Good to Love
FKA twigs

If You Let Me
Sinead Harnett, GRADES

This is What it Feels Like
Banks

Strangers
Halsey, Lauren Jauregui

Hallucinations
dvsn

If Only
Raveena

Fool of Me
Meshell Ndegeocello

Cool Side of the Pillow
Kyle Dion

Bad Blood
Nao

Think About Me
dvsn

Changed- Uncut
Maxwell

Could've Been
H.E.R., Bryson Tiller

Happy Without Me
Chloe x Halle, Joey Bada$$

Officially Missing You
Tamia

Brokenhearted
Brandy, Wanya Morris

Another Lifetime
Nao

Miss You
Gabrielle Aplin

libra season

LIBRA SEASON (INTRO)

the cards read me and told me
balance
and when I asked about you
the seven of coins
winked at me and said
sacrifice   challenge   choose love
find balance

when I weigh myself on my scale
and light my incense
I feel both heavy and wealthy
and when I walk away from the screen
I see a cyberthot deserving of love
and more than you gave

EPIPHANY

my feet were not made for satin
they were not made for dancing freely
they are flat and narrow and hard-bottomed
from all the walking to places I didn't choose
they told me I couldn't dance for so long
and I believed them and stilled my body
my mouth still moved

two left feet, they said
repeated it jokingly
but I didn't get the joke

when I waltzed onto that stage
under the flashing lights
in that empty daytime room
the shame I felt was palpable
a different kind of nakedness
but I caught the rhythm
and suddenly I was beautiful

when I get naked for you
you will marvel at my grace
my big feet pointed toward the ceiling
face down/ass up
you will tip me my dollars
only assholes throw change on the stage
you will ask me my name

and I will lie

you don't deserve to know me.

libra season

libra season

AS FOR MY GIRLS, I'LL RAISE THEM TO THINK THEY BREATHE FIRE.

—Jessica Kirkland, My Girl

libra season

RESTING BITCH FACE

mo/fatcake/dewbaby/all sisters lined up in a row/army style abuse

stand up straight/why are you looking at me like that?/oh, so you bold, huh?/you big and bad, huh?/you think you can take me?/oh, so you think you can beat my ass?/well, you lookin at me like you think you can beat my ass/don't look at the floor, LOOK AT ME/oh, so you think you can beat my ass?/so then why are you lookin at me like that, lil bitch?/you think you know everything but, lookatme, you think you know everything but I'm grown/you can read all the little books you want to/I don't care/you walk around here with your nose in the air looking all high and mighty/like yo shit don't stank/I'm tired of it/mwehmwehmwehmweh, why you whispering?/speak up!/tsk, that's what I thought/you don't have shit to say to me

seventeen/i went to a "real" college

I didn't even write about the girls/i was too afraid that you would read them/I remember when you read fatcake's journal and taunted her/dirty bitch/fat pig/dyke/little slut/these are things you said to her/so i hid mine in the crawl space during the day/moved it and slept on top of it/stuffed it in my bookbag or under my mattress/to keep you out of my thoughts/when I wanted to wear tampons/you questioned my virginity/seventeen/you said i couldn't stay/community college isn't real college, you said/who could you tell about your fallen former golden child?/community college?/in my name/coerced into a private loan/ask your aunt for her information, you said, after we tried you, then gramma/house phone in my name n shit/it's my fault now/you found my condoms when i visited from college/and said it/whore

seventeen/fatcake went to the national guard

I never called you a bitch, you said/but you did/you did/of all the fabulations/of all the fabrications/bitches, you said/you said it/maybe you didn't mean it/but you said it/who alone knew how to make us crumple up inside/you gave fatcake a black eye and told her that she was named after one of her father's whores/she was eight/i was nine/she sprouted too fast and you remember being skinny like your favorite daughter/you called her a dyke when she said she wanted to go to an all-girls school/why do you want to go there? you said/because because i don't want the boys to look at me/and you called her a dyke/ she bound her chest with a series of brassieres and sports bras/ she was more well-endowed than the rest of us/her body was an insult/you picked at her until she had nothing left/and now you tell her to forget/get over it/eighteen years of conditioning/ you took their cell phones and dropped them off near a cornfield/ threw the keys at me/go get them/you said that/you did that

you said you had your mother's children/just like your domineering contrarian nerdy brother (mo)/just like your filthy incompetent lazy brother (fatcake)/just like you/you said: nobody is perfect/fix your face/you said/our fear and hurt visible on our faces angered you/and dewbaby rebelled/got her nails done/got her hair laid/was, naturally, everything you never were, and that's okay/but not for you/she was popular and light skinned and not-brown/you regret having "mixed" children/you regret having daughters/running, running away from you/the problem is having daughters/they said/sluts/bitches/whores/dykes/
fast little girls

eighteen/dewbaby left and never came back

and now you wanna know us.

THE CULT OF UNBOTHEREDNESS

what is feeling?
we don't know her

our hearts are permafrosted semi-precious stones
we have greased our granite faces & bound our serpentine plaits
seven auras, seven radiances, seven terrors
seven stormy splendors to make you suffer

gang gang surfing thru constellations on the back of a pegasus
heading a V-formation with my sisters-in-arms
the strong one, the crying one, the reluctant leader
flying over the threatening sea

we three are lunar risers with divine eyes
we three are monsoons, we are hurricanes
we three are cruel, we are knife-tongued & razor-witted
we are sharp with wet, open, violent mouths

chanting over insult: "it's just a bundle of branches"
even tho we know
words cupped steaming full of chunky crystal falling from the sky
can be murderous

we turned stainless steel into a looking glass
funneling our feelings down labyrinthine brain channels
carved by grotesque memories
put your heart in a mason jar so i can float it, sis

we buy cheap vintage pearls & sink them into buttered skin
we memorize all of your sequin-studded maneuvers
and pretend our arteries are flooded with tumbling ruby cells
while our hearts are sailing, sinking beyond the shore.

ADVENTURES IN PORNOLAND

and that's where the hunger first formed

in high school it was lesbian porn
and thin porcelain sapphic beauties
can't-tell-her-age nubile nymphettes
just barely older than me
made for queerphobic men who love femme but hate femininity

grandmothers who slumber early and late
I crept into the computer room and rubbed one out at the desk
stacked my AOL disk collection, cleared browsers
cleared the history, cleared the cache
can't let sex pop up on my gramma, y'know?
kids aren't supposed to be sexual, y'know?
it's too…human.
too…adult.

don't get caught

down the rabbithole
tiptoeing through the empty house searching
while my parents and sisters are at Sam's Club
nestled in a cardboard box that only professional snoopers
would notice
I searched for clues to understand my grandmother better
journals, smells, old medicine, infomercial buys,
greeting cards tucked away
my gramma is a magpie (a Level 2 hoarder)
instead of history I found treasure
lo! in a cardboard box tucked next to the big tv
which will never move because it is too heavy
there they are in my prepubescent paws:

black bricks of pornographic gold
the women
the women
the women
mouths in a perpetual pout
no one was ugly here
no one is ugly in the bedroom

I think I took my own virginity
the speck of blood on my finger was only slightly alarming
cumming was dazzling
—I didn't know I could do that myself, tame the swelling
make myself see patchy ceiling stars
It was mine to take,
a penetration of self.
Virginity isn't a moment,
issa a gradual siphoning away of innocence

I wanna cum like the first time I came
violently and with a drop of red giant blood on my middle finger
unpublished pussy pulsating with
joy relief tenderness forbiddeness as I
circled my most sensitive spot with
untrained fingermotion

rewind
the distant upclose whirring of the VHS tapes as I
listened for the click of locks in the door
and carefully timed my release

INTO WONDERLAND

At eleven years old
I explored the body of a young girl friend
during a sleepover
her pits had a new musk to them
breasts soft and uninitiated
a womanhood not yet
fully formed

We crawled under the bed and made a cave
in the darkness
she led my fingers, traced her areolas
one-by-one
gently cradled my head as I lowered my face
breath quickening as my lips grazed her belly
we giggled silently

I nuzzled my nose in her new smell and briefly attempted to mimic
the blaxploitation lesbian goddesses I had seen on tape

But really, I just wanted to inhale her

Is your god watching me tangle my fingers
in wisps of uncombed pubic hair?
is your god watching me
gently spread-
pause

You hear sumn?

IF YOU SEE ME, WEEP (HUNGER STONE)

you don't understand my hunger
it stems from can't
canna, I cannaaa
get these voices out of my head that tell me
I'm not good enough
I'm not enough enough
Scrawled on notebook paper
I am famished but eager to prove something
to myself.

We would wake up to dishes on the floor
slick with grease and food socked away,
forbidden until we were faint with exhaustion from cleaning
Boredom punctuated by the song of my mind
Potpourri and yelling piercing my eardrums
as I dreamt of being a ballerina
Pointed my untrained toes
With fallen arches sans flexibility
As I pranced around rhythmless.
Who do you think you are?
                                        nobody

I be my own family
Where prostitute is not an insult
where I can hoe to my heart's content
where I can hoe behind frosted invisible glass
where you and yours can't touch me
They said to do it for the blood
do it for the culture
I am starving, I am homeless, I am ill
I am counting counting counting
I am chanting by the river

I want some water and a new frock designed by the
in-house seamstress to cover my dark marks
I want some rhythm infused by the lessons from

pussypoppin lifegiving splitserving

Fetish Diamond Stallion Laylow
I wanna sweep my sweat-drenched dollars from the stage
It's poking, baby, it's peeking out, ooh

I can't point my toes like you
I can't split & dip & strike a pose
but I can get up on a stage and be seen
Naked
Raw
Titties exposed
Yes, mama, I am hungry for the Love
that wars inside of me
When I look in my mirror
I only see Me
on a stage in front of the judges
giving it all away
making you see
who am I.

BITTER BITCH

I have a mean face
                what that mean?
it means my face don't perform when it's sposed to
it means I'm not smilin when they want me to
it means they looked at me and saw their own lack reflected
back and it made them sad, so they beat me
                            metaphorically speaking
yes, bitch I'm bitter like
dark chocolate cocoa chichory
like summer breakups & fresh-shaven ginger
green tea till you put some honey in me
a bitch is a glass of French Malbec
my innards are fields of dandelion, baby
stew me up with seasoning & plant me in your cheeks
chew me slowly, I'm here to be savored
eat my bitter ass with Chianti, ya bish

why niggas think bitter is an insult? yes, bitch i'm bitter like
arugula, brussel sprouts, roll me up in butter, salt & pepper me
yellow rind grapefruit, dig into me with a spoon
let me gag you
bring me some bittersweet coffee,
                      nigga
workaholic's lifeblood next to an Addy
bitter like sadness coiled up in ya chess
bitter like winter
or bruise-colored eggplant
fo that ass

thanks.

HOW TO MAKE A VILLIAN

mood:
give them a tragedy
make it real, it gotta be real
tellem how often we were up at night,
Listening for the jingle of keys & shifting locks
with Vick's on our upper lips, in our nostrils
& bruises on our *nalgas*
in flannel pajamas
tellem how we prayed nightly
crying to worldly gospel until our eyes were dry
after being beaten in succession
by our mother's deacon boyfriend

make them deformed
inward or outward, it don't matter
stress their deviance, stress their anger
make it seem misplaced, make them seem displaced
don't probe into it unless backstory provides exposition, bby

make them just real enough but still
fundamentally wrong
make them rooted in wrong
but never explain exactly what wrong is
give them a goofy goal and make them explain it
only a moron would spend time on a soliloquy
when it's clearly time to execute
make them supergenius evil intellectuals
who can't seem to get out of their mother's basement
or beat the super everyman hero
make them dark, make them queer
make us believe that dissenters all have a fatal flaw
make them deranged, make them traumatized
stress their damage, what's your damage?

you chaotic good, or chaotic neutral?
you lawful? you cynical, daring, poor?

libra season

are you anti-capitalist?
are you righteously disillusioned?

big mood:
make their pain theatre
give them a reason to be angry
make them abused or poor or Black
then tellem their reason isn't reason enough
make it a franchise, make it a shame we can't be civilized
            and tell us the right way to achieve revolution
            without fucking up the mood.

libra season

"...SHE DID NOT BELIEVE THAT THE WORLD WAS A VALE OF TEARS BUT RATHER A JOKE THAT GOD HAD PLAYED AND THAT IT WAS IDIOTIC TO TAKE IT SERIOUSLY IF HE HIMSELF NEVER HAD."

–Isabel Allende, The House of the Spirits

libra season

BECOMING (THE DRAGON'S DAUGHTER)

I.
Carefully, you weave cotton floss
In-between knit & purl teeth like broken windows
Your sinuses hum with pain
You are salivating & heaving in front of the mirror
You lean forward
and spit into the sink
Two shimmering welo opals
Play-in-color, precious fire
Your nose is dripping chartreuse mucus.

You are a late bloomer
Normally a dragonesse emerges during pre-pubescence
Your period showed late too, around fourteen
You are in your late twenties and suddenly you are

        levitating

and sweating infinitesimal diamonds from your pores
Your plasma is microscopic claret rubies
You fascinate and dazzle
But only yourself and I
You have become a recluse
And stability is your only treasure

II.
There are myriad creation stories
In one a voiceless girl is trapped in an unsatisfying duality with
A nigga too dickmatized (besotted) to recognize or seek
power thru liberation.

Lucifer, black bird of the gods
wingéd & rebellious & accomplished at spellcraft
loathed the floating celestial menagerie, which was full of experiments
made by faithless gods.

Lucifer saw discontent in little Lilith, she offered her Language and Signs,
that which can never be mastered.
Lilith shared these gifts with her little brother Adam,
who turned new words over in his mouth

     like polished stones.
Lilith recited the words for freedom
And Adam said: *What is there to be free from?*
and mocked her.

Lucifer asked: *What is it you desire most?*
Lilith answered: *To change. To leave.*
Lucifer responded: *You can do that. Reach for the words.*
   Lilith stretched.

   Lilith became a phoenix and soared
Left Adam behind in that gilded cage
     She knew what it was
Lilith has a three-inch clit to be sucked on
She is the mother of bad bitches
She is the patron saint of girl dicks
She is the righteous bird of sorrow
She is Promethean flames
She is Oshun's play cousin
Lilith became a Phoenix and re-creates herself

      endlessly

Why are you telling me this? I said.
Because Lilith is the mother of dragons, you said.

III.
Your teeth are falling out—it's the dragon in you
Your mother was born with skin the color of malachite
Your skin has a jade moss tinge to it; glazed obsidian that is now
Cracking open and flaking away like cradle cap
Revealing smooth new skin dipped in shimmering indigo

You are growing your third set of teeth & I have covered the mirrors
so that you can properly mourn your past self
The nubs on your back that you were born with are glazed
with fresh pus and mucus
What am I becoming? You sob into my chest.

   You are becoming what you already are, I say.

And I rock you gently

You are young in both witch and dragon years
You know nothing of your other parent
You were born of an incantation
An invocation from the heart, from my heart
Will I be big like you? you ask.
Only time will tell.

Mama, she whispers, and it is still sweet almost thirty years in:
Who is the mother of witches?

Let me finish the story, dear one.

IV.
Adam only wanted to grow, so Lucifer gave him that, and left
to attend to other godly matters.

And Adam alone was the only being in the garden with Language,
and no one to share with.
Until a curious young god,
sensing anguish matching their own
appeared and set up shop. Taught Adam all the maneuvers of loving
with your body and raw ambrosia.
Adam, enthralled, did not understand the ways of gods.

The little god didn't want Adam the way Adam wanted him
   Only him.
Man was of the gods but the gods were not of man. The little
god could not abide the stagnancy of mere mortals; THEY
preferred the fluidity of the divine.
Adam prostrated himself, so obedient, so sprung,
caked up mud on his knees,
  he pleaded.
But THEY couldn't give him what he desired;
Adam, though beloved, was not a god.
  Please don't leave me, Adam cried.
The little god conferred with the other gods, who chastised THEM.
They blamed Lucifer for offering Language;
  why give pets the ability to dissent?
Lucifer offered them the gift of selfishness
She told them it was perfectly permissible to ask for what they wanted
Lilith, Adam, and Ava's interactions with the divine had taught
them to desire.

The gods offered a solution: to make another being to sate Adam's appetite.
A cruelty, to give humans all the qualities & ambition of birds,
with no wings for flight or fury.
For gods are mutable, shifting from one form or gender to another
Shaping themselves like sculptors
Becoming whatever our eyes desire

They said: *Make him a counterpart, whatever.*
Then maybe they will breed and leave us be.
They said: *This is your project, now stop bothering us.*
You are growing too old for indecisiveness.

The little god cracked THEIR knuckles and got to work
The method was trickier without Lilith—Adam was Lilith's
fraternal twin (in a manner of speaking), duplicated then re-
formed in an image that pleased the gods
The little god didn't want to bother the wayward child, Lilith
Who had become less human than Adam anyway,
So THEY began from scratch
And Adam turned away, ashamed by his loneliness and want
Want of power to shape destinies
Want of godliness to pluck that god
     right from THEIR lofty perch
Lust for things he did not understand.
He turned his back to the young god's swift angular hand motions.

And out of the ether, Ava emerged.

V.
I am Dusk.
I am changing.
My skin is indigo, dotted with rarefied constellations
I wonder: *Who but your creator will love you when you're blue?*
My mother, a pure dragon, told me all the tales as a young girl
How Lilith, fiery, sat on a moon and whispered to it,
till it cracked like an egg
And the First Dragon erupted, coral and radiant
I marveled at my new wings
as they burst forth from my shoulder blades
My mother rubbed the joints and coaxed them out
It was painful
It was like giving birth

As they slowly peeled from their membranes and unfolded
Into the night sky
My new teeth are coming in
They are hard and capable
My mother bathed me
And rubbed my scalp while I closed my eyes

VI.
But the little god continued to visit Adam.
Ava wandered in the garden while they danced, ignoring her.
She followed the birds and learned how to Sing
She learned their Language in secret
She deftly tracked the little god and Adam
And watched them rut and grunt and mouth forbidden words, her eyes wide with revelation.
Adam's throat, raw and exposed, as he threw his head back
Sweat beading along his arched spine.
Ava gazed in wonder and silence.

Little gods are even more fickle than elder gods.
THEY grew tired of slumming it in the garden,
and announced THEIR departure... after one last tryst.

Adam, in his fury at the god's abandonment,
spat hot semen onto the ground
And screamed at the top of his lungs
And the god turned Adam away with finality
Dick limp with satiety,
And returned to the heavens.
Gods are notorious for their callousness in affairs.
They move from one planet to the next,
and take and leave what they covet.

Ava attempted nurturing Language, mimicking the little god,
      to soothe Adam,
    but he remained inconsolable,

        staring at the sky.

Adam begged for his celestial lover
He raged and rejected Ava
He cried like a wounded animal in the darkness

He raped her and shouted to the sky
As if only he had been harmed
How he profusely pleaded for his humanity
While violating her

Ava was named after a bird by a fanciful young god
Who hadn't the prudence or kindness
to give their new pet the gift of her namesake,
Preferring to keep them locked in a floating nursery
just beneath the god's palace, edging a precipice

VII.
Glittering reptilian sapphires have erupted all over my body
Once I got to my mid-twenties I was convinced I would never change
But of course, that was folly
My teeth are crystallized diamonds
My tongue is coated in gold leaf
My mother says: *Dragons are of the sky, they are of fire.*
This is why we are made of living jewelry
We have no need for most earthly delights
Though they offer us much comfort
We are our own treasure and have no desire to search for more

VIII.
Lilith was Adam's equal but Ava was Adam's possession
And possessions cannot leave; they can only be discarded
So she stayed with Adam who beat her brutally
For not being the lover he so desperately desired
And Ava wept and slashed her wrists
and begged for relief

Lucifer returned from a long business trip and intervened
She fluttered down to Ava and healed her wounds
Kissed her in the center of her body
Stitched her up, and fed her Light and Magic
Luci, Ava said, *I want to make something.*
Lucifer smiled knowingly: *I can give you that.*
She gave Ava her book of shadows and secret signs
And showed her the earth beneath the floating garden
Lucifer became Ava's mate and knew her
And Ava swelled up after that and glowed golden
and licked the fruit juice from Lucifer's fertile fingertips
And Ava was shielded by Lucifer from Adam's violence.

And Adam was entombed in his fury.

Adam appealed to the little god one last time.
And the little god saw what THEY had done
and was ashamed.

The little god, angry at Lucifer's interference,
jealous that THEIR pets were not predictable,
and frightened by Adam's behavior,
conferred with more experienced gods
Who nodded and summoned Lucifer,
who fought for them fiercely,
even Adam.
But Lucifer had defied the elder gods by teaching Ava sorcery.
In the end, she accepted her fate
The elder gods clipped her wings and
banished her from the heavens.
Upon her departure Lucifer looked back and quietly stated:
There is more than one way to fly.

The elder gods located Adam and put him in a coma to rest.
What of Lucifer and Ava? said the little god.
But the elder gods shook their heads.
One spoke: *Little god, you let your fleshly desires*
get the best of you, and now you
must also be punished. But not Ava.
Another: *Ava desires freedom, and Lucifer has decided.*
They muttered amongst themselves and nodded in unison:
Let the earth be their wings.
And they banished the young foolish god.

The little god then visited Ava and Lucifer,
saw their love and their light,
Ava's halfmoon-belly; a new creation
And the little god felt THEIR malice melt away
and told the couple about the elder gods' decision
That THEY would be the one to lead them from the garden
Never to return
For that was their gift and punishment.
    Lucifer demurred.
But Ava brightened at the prospect of a new adventure
Beyond the verdant prison and its faux protection.
Ava said: *There is enough love for all three of us, I think.*

libra season

Lucifer said: *Promise you never harm another being again,*
and we will go willingly.

And the little god agreed, gratefully.
And Lucifer put a mark on the little god's forehead,
and sealed the promise in blood.
Then Lucifer hoisted Ava up on her back and said: *Prepare the way.*

I am afraid to fly
But my mother is not a god
And thus, she coaxes me out onto the wind
And watches me take flight

So the little god opened up the gates
And the triad leapt over the edge into the world

And it was good.

WHAT IMMA DO (INTERLUDE)

I'mma put you in my mouf
You got a little beard hanging wet & glistening like moonshine
from the back
Two fingers of
                ice
                          warm
                                      bourbon

    I'm gonna
    I'm gonna
    I'm gonna

Kneel at your feet &
kiss them
Wash them
Paint them

Notes of exaltation will
Overwhelm you into my bed
I won't let your evil whimpering silence
Get into my head no more

I'mma do it
I'mma stumble right into your magic
I'mma make you
Put it on the line
Witchy bitch

libra season

WATERLOGGED

what magic are you to have me
splayed out in my bed and
rearranged to
poetry
and
incense
and
pleasure-pain
as you
drip

           drip

                      drip

oil
down
my
      spine

your mouth said: *i want to carry you*
you will always have a home with me.

glug

I don't believe you
people who have wings
carry the spirit of leaving
in their bones
and I am my own coven

glug

what sorcery is this?

glug

your fingers twist in my marsh at high tide
you feel more familiar than my Familiar

libra season

my wetness is my betrayal
that shuh shuh shuh of my
wanting to cum for you
the pitter-patter of my lower heart
your mouth is
poised
pursed
puckered
perched

glug

but if you just
let me

glug

underwater
I am a trap mermaid, without a sea to siren
you took one of your heart-jewels &
traced my clavicle gently and
thrust it into the cavity in my chest
like a dagger in dragon form
I am flushed and overwhelmed at your

glug

magic sans formation
your lack of formal magical education
how did I let you
come
this
close?

glug
glug
gulp
gasp

libra season

I'm not ready for absolution
just yet.

WATER CHALLENGE

I am the sufferer of a curious affliction
a hydrological imbalance,
a water supply shortage of epic proportions
Ion have no tears left to cry
—not due to my aquagenic urticaria
                                       but simply cuz
                                       I've cried too often
                                       and suffered for it;
the effects: a bothersome array of crimson wheals
sprouting up and peppering my supple sage skin

         any time water touches me
I break out and shrivel up like a green rind
         ain't that fucked up, G?
bein a trap mermaid trapped
moored in a country that places
                                       emerald-skinned stunnas like me
at the bottom of the social ladder

I like to lay in the bottom of the shower sometimes
and let the rain fall down on me
as I grit my teeth and curse my body
while imagining what it's like to only die once

this day
I had been invited to eat
She invited *me*
so I applied my emulsion cream,
doused myself in Florida Water and
dripped rosehip oil onto my face
stared at my puffy eyes in the mirror
         as the Cat prowled in the hallway
mewling and asking me when I'll back

         I don't fucking know.

She is a glittering dragonesse
who drew the Cat's interest initially
but she chose me
and I have to know why
the cards were unclear on anything but
some sort of cosmic connection
and I'm late
my hair a mess
a scarf
a word
a prayer

I walked into the restaurant lookingfeelingbreathing like
                              magic
she gushed and I felt myself flinch
her skin was smokey, verdigris, a darker green than mine
she had similar scars but her bags were lighter
she was all fire
                          I flinched
she was all stars
                          I flinched
she was all steel
                          I tasted metal on my tongue

her gaze was like a baby's—wide and questioning and dancing
foolish lullabies
alien enthusiasm
arrogance
You think the world can't touch you? I thought
You think you're better than me? I thought
I frowned, her sinewy wings twitched when she giggled, and I
felt the urge to rip them off
peel them slowly like puss-flooded scabs only half-formed
I can fly too, I thought
and she said out loud: *we should fly together*

libra season

libra season

"THIS IS WHY YOU SHOULDN'T FALL IN LOVE, IT BLINDS YOU. LOVE IS WICKED DISTRACTION."
—Gregory Maguire,
Wicked: The Life and Times of the Wicked Witch of the West

A DATE & A DRAGON

I planned a date for us because I am a hoarder
I took notes all covert n shit
You would say something you thought was mundane
I would scribble it down or commit it to memory
You are a fucking jewel but you are not pyrite-shiny
You are crystalline Indian Water magic
And I am a dragon, all air and fire and magpie-like
Snorting plumes of smoke as you run your fingers through my braids
Together we are riches, alone we are ruins

You walked into my cave and sat down among my many memories
I thought you came to stay so I cleaned up a little
I wanted to make you comfortable
You like to walk in your bare feet like me so it was easy for me to welcome you
Please sit down, please lay down, please close your eyes,
Please breathe

I want you to be rich with me
I want you to be free with me
I am a dragon
I want you to fly with me
I want you to do whatever you want to do
Even if it means that you leave one day

I wanted to take you to a wooded valley and get your feet off the ground
So you could see what it's like to be me
I wanted to give you the jewels off my back—I don't need them, really
You are the only jewel I need and I will wear your memory like an omega chain
I will wear you like *una cadena de oro* from the gods

You said you read me, you said our ancestors brought us together
I want to believe you, so I do

Let me take you for a walk,
Let us go down by the lake with our candles
And sit in our sacred circle

Let us sacrifice,
Me first, me first
I am a dragon
I am big, I am clumsy, but my heart is softer than my skin
I am a gentle dragon when I have no enemies

You are a diviner
Your heart is a geode I want to crack
I just know there is tourmaline in there, amethyst maybe
Your feet are feldspar, your pussy is apatite, your face granite
--but your insides are magma, like mine.
Your navel is a pearl and your cheeks are garnet-flushed
Your tongue is jade, your lips are lapis
And your fingertips are imperial topaz
Let's play, I said, and you humored me
Who can resist a dragon?

You are a nomad at heart, a wanderer,
I liked to enjoy the time I had with you
The wild dragon in me wants to follow you wherever you go
But you are not my only treasure
And I am slightly more domesticated than you
I don't want to bother you but can I take you on a date?

I just feel like if we could do this one thing, on one night
that I will never have regrets about anything
I am not your only lover, but I feel alone in your eyes
I feel navy blue
I feel purple
I feel like a solo artist on the stage of you
Sleek, glimmering, big & brave
I never want to say goodnight to you

My scales are actually soft, if you want to touch them
People think I am hard, they see me and they run away
I try very hard not to breathe fire in their direction
I want to be polite
But sometimes I get so excited at the prospect of companionship
I don't know my own strength

libra season

I was born a dragon but I could never fly
until I left home and shed my second skin
Did you know dragons could do that? Well, they can.
They put me in a cage sometimes, but you never did,
And I'm grateful
I have more than one heart
Did you know that dragons have multiple hearts?
Well, they do, and I took one of them and put it in a carved wooden
jewelry box that was stained with the blood of my enemies
I never forgive unless I forget
My mind is elephantine
You say it's a flaw, I call it strategy

We agree to disagree

I have friends, but I don't have you
and you are the candy house of my
tall tales, danger and allure and
heart-breaking, egg-cracking silence.
I was so comfortable in my skin
But suddenly my scales seem shinier,
They glitter like molten honey
And made you feel dull in comparison.

You are a witch
and all witches have feline familiars
It was a stray but you gave it a home
And suddenly it could not survive without you
Cats see themselves as gods do,
they are envious and spiteful and manipulative,
the dark side of cleverness
In their mind, *you* belong to *them*.
It envied our love and our time and
it plotted against us
It curled itself around your neck when I would visit
And it would burst into my cave and enviously nip at your waist
when you fell asleep on my belly
I love cats, but your Cat hates me

It scratches my things when we let it into my cave
so we outlawed it to the valley beyond and when you leave me,
you greet it in your chromatic glass house beneath
the willow tree.

After weeks of planning I concocted a spell
—I am not a witch, it took me time to get the incantation just so
You appeared one day with a long gash on your forearm
An augury of what was to come
You insisted you were fine but rage bubbled inside me
I licked the crimson tears and cerise blossoms sprouted where
my tongue passed over your lustrous skin
You whimpered and moaned and told me not to worry, don't worry
I am a witch, you say, *I am a conjurer*
I don't know anything about your kind of magic
So I brooded silently, and smelled your hair, wrapping you in my smoke
My body is a furnace and you sleep with me the way an infant sleeps
on its mother's chest with milk on its mind and calm on its breath
I am a dragon, I know how to love

Things began to go missing.

I never blamed the cat. I pretended not to notice, but you confronted it
It wrapped itself around your legs and hissed bottomless denial
It whispered lies to me in my sleep
You are a desert, you are fallow, you are meaningless to her
Neither you nor she are the magic; I am the magic
It left hexes in my garden and pissed on my herbs for the villagers
It grinned in the darkness and meowed menacingly
She is mine, it said, and I didn't disagree
I am a dragon, I own no one, and no one owns me

Cat tongue, cat lies scrawled on bits of parchment
imbued with energy it stole from you
It placed a bewitched dagger in the heart I gave you
and counted three times, three lies
My number is four, so it affected me
but you were able to mend me for the time being
You sent the Cat away and beckoned me into your crystal lair

libra season

I became small and laid your head in my lap and stroked your curls
While tears ran down your cheeks and singed your skin
You needed mending too
I know minor feline charms,
I am a trained soothsayer
I purred pruriently, I administered an ancient dragon remedy,
I knelt and placed my snout at your altar and consulted my book of shadows, strategies of allurement and horoscopy
You wanted the stars to be just so but I stopped caring
You are a need, you are magnetism, you are cardinal air to my ember
I am a dragon and I am danger, risk, brio and luxury
Sweep from right to left, knock eleven times, cut the deck twice

Regret is foreign to me
Dragons don't regret, they act
Dragons *are* action, they *do*
Eye think
I am life personified
And you are a witch
Balanced & imbalanced

We spent three days until the Cat returned
I left disheartened and disheveled

What of our date?
What of the diary of promises and poetry I meant for you?
What of the lake and our sacrifices?
I roared in violent protest and you said I was
    monstrous
You said you knew I didn't mean it but you were frightened of me
I was too big, too intense
My scales were too glossy
and I took up too much space in your crystal house
Cats are smaller, cats are shapeshifters
And I am just a dragon
I shed another skin—I didn't mean to
But sudden fasting from love clawed away will do that
I don't understand your kind of magic
I don't understand Cat magic

libra season

Paw prints replace the geraniums and dahlias that sprung up under the soles of your sooted feet on the walking path to my cave
I pull my cards now and think of you in the sky,
your curved fairy feet dangling from your broom under a titian moon
I cannot bear to think of my heart in that box
I reached for my own magic and removed the dagger myself
I never forgive unless I forget

I am a dragon.

SPEAK EASY

while skimming a Midsummer Night's Dream on the train after grocery shopping, and thinking of you.

how do I unremember your careful moans
                              down there?
I couldn't cum or stop thinking long enuf to
cum for you
that fucked up shit you said was on my mind
& I couldn't believe in your touch
couldn't believe your mouth
a crisis of faith
pretty words breed pretty lies
did you
did you mean it
when you said you loved me?

rambling, I'm rambling
—lovers and madmen have such seething brains
we said things just to unsay them
and didn't say the things we needed to say
maybe it was unneeded
probably it was nobody's fault
probably

if I speak it soft, will you hear me then?

is it possible that something of you is
twined around my heart?
is it possible that our silences were
too bloated
too violent
too real
too full of the possibility of
letting go of a predetermined destiny of
sad songs, abuse & bad romances
looking for absolution for the sin of being alive

libra season

lulling ourselves into a daily weed-induced stupor

I am vacation bae
an escape from your daily realities
I am the ghost of desires unfulfilled

ours was a lush ivylike private affair
invasive and probing under our skins
you came for me and pushed me away
too much, I'm always too much

starvation is preferable to submersion
you are accustomed to feast or famine
never both at the same time
someone else to fill you while they emptied you

forgive me for speakin outta turn even though
ion forgive nothin and no one.
forgive me for burning you with my heat;
love looks not with the eyes, but with the mind
too much sunlight on your pretty little blooms
forgive me for spoiling your garden that day
shoulda done this more gradually
but I was so eager to love you
I didn't see you burning, smoldering away.

forgive my hasty retreat
forgive my lack of forgiveness
forgive my inability to love you
the way you needed me to.

phone calls on the regular
something about this shit makes me wanna
call you up
something about this shit makes me wanna
run through your garden
erect a gazebo
build you a moat
tend to you

water you the way I used to.
I used to sit at your feet and trace the curves of your
ballerina arches
ignoring the soot on your soles.
your thighs smelled of incense and floral waters
I used to
say the right things
I used to
speak gently to you
when I couldn't hold you in my arms
I made my words a soft bed for you to lie in
and glazed them with honey for you to sample

I know you don't need me
but
did you ever want me?
don't answer that
you don't owe me nothing
and I damn sure don't owe you
not even my silence
so why am I mad?
where were the words when I had the time?
where were the words when I had the range?
I ran and I ran and I ran
Out of words
Out of fear
Out of sheer exhaustion

I never expected you to beg me to stay.

I never expected to leave.

I—
I'll never forget your taste
You clenched up when I reached for you at first
You said you were embarrassed of your openness
But you wanted to cum for me.

I licked my coated fingertips & it was easier than I thought

libra season

To reach for the action to express
This bottomless well of confusion
To coax you closer
To stick my nose and my tongue in & lap up your frustration
To have you swallow your voice

Say it again
Say that you love me again
Say that
Say that thing
Or say nothing at all

CAKE CITY

dulce, do you miss me when you're out
eating fancy pussy in extravagant warehouses
with soft beating notes punctuating manufactured silence
while you dust your palms on shortening butterthicc batter thighs
& fill your mouth with that porous structure?
do you ever think of me as you flounce thru the city
on baking soda air dazzling the clowns with your
piel canela, vanilla eyes & chemical magic?

do you ask permission before you gently slide your fork into it?
after removing it from the hot oven, do you make sure to give it the gift of Air
& sprinkle confections, squeezing out every bit of frosted loneliness
onto the warm-cooled stacked surface?
do you miss me coming to your bakery?

do you lick the frosting first before diving in
or do you take cake & frosting into your mouth all at once & scarf it down?
do you savor them the way you savored me?
do you survey their stacked up sweets with those same eyes?
do you put them away nicely in the dish?
or do you taste & throw away their excess the way you did mine?
do you ever wake up with taste rememories of me
cocoalifted, moist, babysauf & frustrated
on your tongue, or do you do your best to digest
last night's dessert?

WEAPONS

oh, so we weaponizing
a goofy, prickly-haired cactus bitch is staring back at me
segmented eyes blinking
one-then-two-then-fourrr.
my hair is *de la fleur* rebellious realness
my skin is green scratches, scales verdigris stormed
iridescent eyemeat buggin out under the graced ledge of my brow
peeking, I'm piquing, I'm pea-king
king of this bathroom
king of the Nile
bitch watch me land watch me buzzzz
watch me circle the steam-blanketed room
watch me press up against the smokey glass &
smeeeeear my itchy palms against it
you, not me
you a reflection of me
you not real, you a wanna-be
bug-eyed cuntiferous bitch I am
watch me gravitate
watch me levitate

my mouth is frothy with bisexual power
bath bomb delight
delicious rotting cavities
watch me yank them out one by one
peep the opaline *naqqārah* swimming
in the palm of my hand while blood trickles
following the graceful line of my jaw
decorating the sink's enamel like margarite
I grit, I grind bones of contention
I said shit y'ain't want me to say
a contrarian soothsayer
watch me file solid gum staying buckteeth to shrill points
watch me be a scarecrow & laugh wickedly
like the threatening holiday you want me to be
watch me aggressively peel off my jelly mask & streeeetch my neck

libra season

peep my blooms, peep my lined prickly pear skin
lookatme I'm so arrogant
listen to my cunty laugh
not a ha-ha or a ki-ki
nigga

watch me towel off, watch me wipe it all away
fuck living out of spite, I live for
your insults missing me, judgment stilled
like an electric bar splayed on basmati
like a crystal ball gone dim
wait till I channel my real words
wait till I get these poems off
wait till I threaten-promise-forget about you
watch me sharpen these syllables
watch me pull these nettles out & make gumdrops out of me
watch me be the uglycute bitch you
aspire to
be

libra season

BLOOD UNDER THE SKIN

blood is thicker than water
but who thicker than you?
Let me feed you egusi with my fingers
curl up around you like a magic shawl
I am a golden goose with a clutch of eggs
You hold me spellbound between your legs
the blood, it was only the blood,
is thicker than water

come in honor of me
I am fire and air and plasma
I won't make you one of my treasures
You deserve more than that
Blood red brick builds up your altar
and you are my private dancer
We are
eating with our hands
boiling
coagulating
reducing the heat and inspecting our armor
It is feeding time
And I have hung up my sword on your wall

now wait
waitwaitwait
your heart said
I can't, my heart
I need I need I need I need
a moment
I slipped right in and I felt myself
I felt her
tighten and curl around my fingers
sopping

it is only the blood, they whispered

libra season

mouthing words I somehow understand
to kneel is to rise in you
drenched in an everlasting
crimson tide
not from battle
but from love

libra season

> "I KNOW STORMS, I KNOW HOW THEY COME UPON YOU!"
>
> — Gregory Maguire, *Wicked: The Life and Times of the Wicked Witch of the West*

libra season

BUT WHEN I GET MY WINGS...

pressed don't even begin to describe this feeling
I am holding up rain like overburdened cumulus
I am monsooning inwardly
I am replaying our last conversations
and feeling thirst
was I always this hungry?
I want
I need
I am mistaken
My ego supplanted my Id
In my quest to love fluidly
I forgot about returns
but when I get my wings
I will forget our quiet mornings
I will forget your feet next to my face
I will forget kissing your ankles and
your sticky-sweet taste
your fingers pressed against the bed
as you murmured and stretched your neck.

It's so silly I know
To want to know for sure
The hunger for reassurance as I set myself
at your feet waiting for you to pet my head
return the warmth I gave
I left notes on your altar with my tongue
Hoping my scriptures would give love
I want to forget the ugliness I felt
when doubt was inserted
and how I will never know
whether you ever thought of me as beautiful
or think of me at all.

libra season

THANK YOU

first, I want to thank myself. you have been thru so much this year, yet you continue to forge ahead. you're amazing and you deserve kisses down low and tickets to a Beyonce concert, but you will have to settle for a bath with a bath bomb and some weed because I'm broke. Ily.

Eme is the best big sister, and friend. she lets me know when I'm doing too much (and just enough, ow) and helped me take this poetry from another, bigger, project, and make it into its own thing. I mothered this project, and she definitely othermothered it. she gave it form and life and dignity, and identified the patterns I was missing. she always calls me on my bullshit, and I am forever grateful.

I am so glad to have sisters. they are the only ones who share some of these memories with me, and I am grateful to know them. thank you, dewbaby, for the long conversations about everything. somehow, you became the middle child, I'm not sure how that happened. thank you to fatcake for giving me permission to detail certain things in my writing. I love you both.

thank you to my ex-partner and very good friend, Malik. he never got tired of me reading these poems to him or bouncing ideas off him in the middle of the night. he was always available for me to cry to and renewed my faith in change, but you niggas still trash though. Malik read these acknowledgements and wants me to mention that he's 5'8", quoting: "Let them know."

thank you to Sasha, Eme, Malik, Zalika, Tally, and Maddy for offering community and support and impromptu counseling sessions. I love y'all and I don't know that I'd have made it thru this year without you. Sasha be knowin. Zalika, thank you for always checking on me and making me feel like my work is important. Thank you for the conversation, for sharing your brilliant thoughts with me, and for pushing for academics to prioritize the voices of Black sex workers. Maddy, thank you for loving me and for letting me be a safe space, however brief it was. you reintroduced me to real life magic. you reintroduced me to vital parts of myself. and I am forever grateful, never regretful, for my time with you.

thank you to all my Twitter peeps who sent money and kind words and love. thank you to everyone who boosts my content and defends me from bullies online. thank you to my gramma for letting me come home again and again, and for (mostly) making her home a safe space for me to escape to. thank you for providing me with a library to admire. your books stacked double and triple deep were always an inspiration. thank you to my mother for gifting me her superb taste in music and giving me a foundation for my phenomenal music taste. thank you to my great aunts for giving me sewing/interior design DIY fever (gramma & Dot), a love of pumps and sequins (Say), and a swift, brandy-laced tongue (alladem).

thank you to Jamilah Lemieux, who bought me my first (pink) Xmas tree since leaving my abuser, and MiniMilah, because she's awesome and iconic, and I know she'll enjoy seeing her moniker in print.

thank you to whoever I didn't name, you are no less important, there's just a fuckton of you who are awesome and I gotta wrap this up.

thank you to my Little Bear, you keep me alive and feeling.

libra season

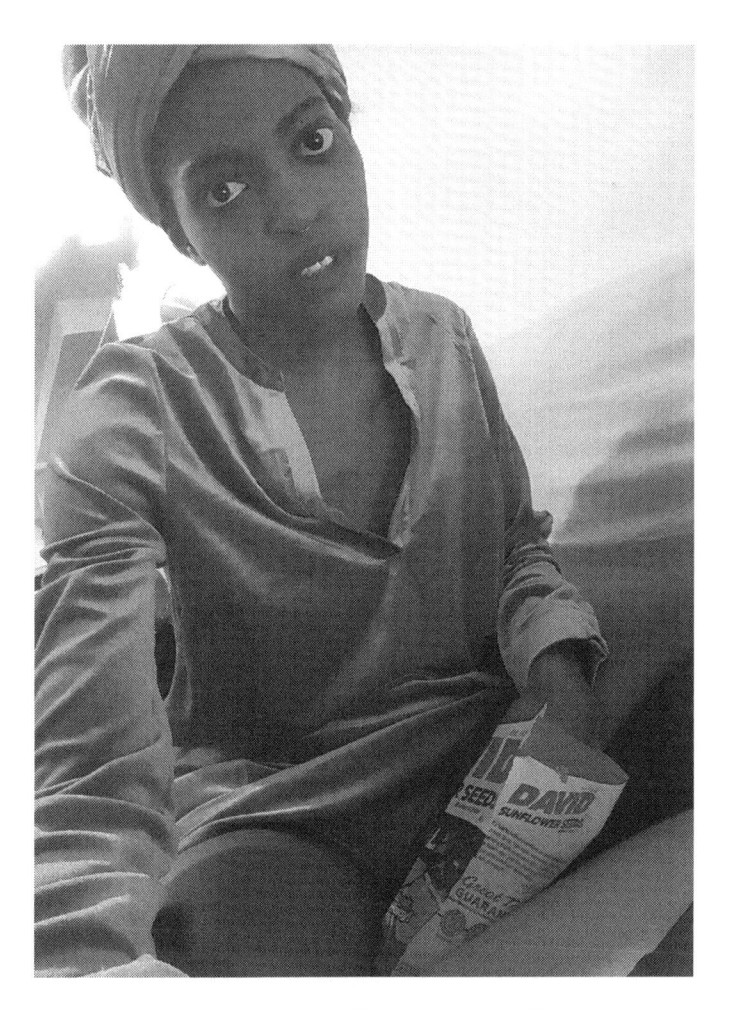

AUTHOR BIO

suprihmbé is a part-time writer, part-time artist, part-time thot, and full-time mother. she has been a sex worker for nearly a decade and has worked as a stripper, adult content creator, and a webcam model, as well as dabbled in escorting, in that time. suprihmbé saw a need for the oft-silenced voices of Black, trans, and/or poor sex workers to be amplified, as well as for sex work to be understood from the perspective of those who are actually in the trade, not anti-sex work groups, or intellectually curious academics. she started bbydoll press to publish lesser known voices, including her own. this is her first book.

libra season

Made in the USA
Middletown, DE
14 January 2019